# Run Little Fawn, Run!

For Linda and John
~S.C.

For Charlotte and David
~G.R.

MAGI PUBLICATIONS
1 The Coda Centre, 189 Munster Road, London SW6 6AW
www.littletigerpress.com

First published in Great Britain 2001
This edition published 2004

Text copyright © Sheridan Cain 2001
Illustrations copyright © Gavin Rowe 2001
Sheridan Cain and Gavin Rowe have asserted their rights
to be identified as the author and illustrator of this work under
the Copyright, Designs and Patents Act, 1988

A CIP catalogue record for this book is available from
the British Library

Printed in Dubai
1 85430 951 X

3 5 7 9 10 8 6 4 2

# Run Little Fawn, Run!

SHERIDAN CAIN

ILLUSTRATED BY GAVIN ROWE

MAGI PUBLICATIONS

LONDON

The sun rose, and Little Fawn
opened his sleepy eyes. He felt
warm and safe, for, as always,
his mother was there to look
after him.

But today Mother Deer said to him gently, "You're a big boy now and you must be brave. I will not always be here, and you must learn to take care of yourself. Come, Little Fawn, I will show you how."

Little Fawn followed his mother through the dark, thick woods until they reached a clearing. At the edge stood a shack that smelled strongly of Man. Suddenly Little Fawn did not feel big or brave.

"Mother," said Little Fawn. "What if Hunter comes with his sack and his fearsome dogs?" "Hunter is clumsy," said Mother Deer, "and his dogs are, too. Your ears are sharp. You will hear him before he sees you. So run then, Little Fawn, for your legs are strong and swift."

Mother Deer led Little Fawn through the
trees to the edge of the woods, where Fox
lay sleeping in the sun.
"Mother," said Little Fawn. "What if Fox
comes prowling? He will gobble me up."

"Fox's teeth are sharp," said Mother Deer,
"but his scent is strong. You will smell
him, Little Fawn. Then you must run,
for your legs are long."

Mother Deer and Little Fawn tiptoed
back into the meadow. Little Fawn
looked all around, and up towards the sky.
"Mother," said Little Fawn, "what if
Eagle spies me with his fine big eyes,
when he soars overhead?"

"When you see Eagle, Little Fawn," said Mother Deer, "you must stay as still as a rock. You must not move so much as an ear. Then he will not see you from the sky."

Mother Deer and Little Fawn
started back towards the herd.
But then they heard a crack
and a snap, and Hunter crashed
through the trees, his dogs at
his side.
"Run, Little Fawn!" cried
Mother Deer.

Mother Deer and Little Fawn ran.
They ran as fast as their strong, long legs
would carry them. They ran as swift as
the wind, through the trees and deep into
the wood. Soon they were out of sight.
Hunter called off his dogs and stomped
away, his sack empty.

He was no match
for Mother Deer
or for Little Fawn.

Though Mother Deer ran fast, Little Fawn
ran faster. Soon he had left Mother Deer
behind, and when he turned to look back,
she was no longer in sight.
"She will come soon," said Little Fawn,
and he lay down to wait for her.

No sooner than he
did so, he heard rustling.
He could not see Fox,
but he could smell his
strong and powerful
scent.

So Little Fawn sprang up again and ran. He ran
as fast as his strong, long legs would carry him.
He darted this way and that, through the trees
and back into the open meadow.

Fox dashed after him, but Little Fawn
was too quick. Soon Fox lay exhausted
in the long grass.
"I'll get you another day," he sulked.

Once again, Little Fawn lay
down and waited for Mother Deer.
He could no longer smell the strong
scent of Fox. He could not hear
Hunter stomping and clomping.
But above him, Little Fawn saw
Eagle with his great wings,
swooping towards him.

For all the world, Little Fawn wanted to run, but he remembered what Mother Deer had told him. He stayed as still as a rock. As Eagle swooped closer, Little Fawn began to tremble. He was sure his ears would twitch.

Closer and closer came Eagle,
until Little Fawn could hear
the beat of his wings. But
Eagle sailed on. He did not
see Little Fawn.

Little Fawn was tired, and grew sleepy
as he waited for Mother Deer to find
him. Then, suddenly, he heard a sound
– a sniffy, snuffly sound – moving towards
him. Little Fawn listened with his sharp
ears. The sound was too dainty for Hunter.
"Oh dear, what shall I do?" thought Little
Fawn. "Should I run, or should I stay?"

Little Fawn sniffed with his sharp nose,
then leapt up from where he was hidden.
Now he knew exactly who it was . . .

"Hello, Mother," cried Little Fawn.
"You've found me at last. But why
are you crying?"
"Because I thought I had lost you,"
said Mother Deer, nuzzling him.
"I did just as you told me," said
Little Fawn. "I'm quite safe."

"And you always will be,"
replied Mother Deer.